Five Tales for Christmas

Bernice Zięba

Jan Webmedia

JAN WEBMEDIA CLASSICS

WORLD FAIRY TALES

English Fairy Tales (Jacobs)
Welsh Fairy Tales (Griffis)
Scottish Fairy Tales (Grierson)
Irish Fairy Tales (Yeats)
Manx Fairy Tales (Morrison)
Christmas Tales (folk tales and famous stories)
Five Tales for Christmas (Zięba)

janwebmedia.uk

Five Tales for Christmas

Written by

Bernice Zięba

Jan Webmedia

Cambridge

ISBN: 979-8363420054

Published by: Jan Webmedia, Cambridge
First edition entitled: *The Three Nuts and Other Christmas Tales,* 2017
Second edition: *Five Tales for Christmas*, November 2022
Book cover design: Jan Webmedia
Formatting: Jan Webmedia

janwebmedia.uk

Contents

THE SHELL GIRL

Once upon a time there was a young girl who lived near the beach on an island, far away. Each morning at sunrise, before the fishermen got into their boats, she collected shells on the beach, which the tide had swept in. She found all sorts of shells. Most shells were white on the inside but some were lined with mother-of-pearl. The young girl was poor—her mother had died a while ago. She looked after her old father, who was a tailor, and she lived in a tiny room under the roof, where she kept her shells in a large chest.

The islanders thought these shells were useless and worthless since countless of them were lying around on the beach, like ordinary stones or like sand. Nobody knew why she was collecting these shells, and people often laughed at her and called her the foolish shell girl.

One day a ship arrived at the shore. No one had ever seen such a ship before. It was larger than a fishing-boat with white sails rising on tall masts. On the ship was a young, handsome Prince from a kingdom the islanders had never heard of. When the Prince stepped ashore they admired his grand blue clothes and his white-feathered hat.

One of his servants announced: "Our Prince is traveling the world in search of a young girl who is pretty, industrious and clever. He has sailed around half the world and has not yet found a suitable girl. Either they were pretty but not clever, or they were industrious but not pretty, or clever but not industrious.

Many mothers were eager to have their daughter married to the handsome Prince. They didn't want to miss the chance of being mother of a Princess. So they bragged and boasted about their daughters to impress the Prince; and the Prince took a good look at each and every one of them. He asked them questions to test their wits and he gave them tasks to fulfil. But again—each and every one of them proved to be unsuitable for the Prince.

Before the Prince gave up, he asked: "Is there any other young girl left on your island, whom I have not met yet?" The mothers all shook their heads and said: "Is it not enough, your majesty? We have presented all our daughters to you, each and every one."

So the Prince ordered the anchor to be pulled up and was ready to sail away. However, before the ship left, he noticed that his blue clothes had become worn out. So he sent a servant back on land to ask if a tailor lived on the island, who could sew a suit that was as blue as the evening sky and as shiny as the stars. The islanders ran to the shell girl's old father, and he approached the ship with a measuring band and blue material to prepare a suit, fit for the Prince.

The tailor soon produced a splendid suit, for he was a skilled and experienced tailor, and he brought the finished suit back to the Prince.

When the Prince examined the suit he said: "This is a fine suit and it's blue like the evening sky, but it doesn't shine like the stars. I will give you time until tomorrow noon to make it shine like the stars."

The tailor bowed in front of the Prince and

hurried home. He sat at the table in his little workshop and held his head in his hands until the shell girl came down from her attic room, ready to clean up the workplace as she always did in the evening. When she saw her father so depressed, she asked him what the matter was.

"I must make this fine blue suit shine like the stars, for that is what the Prince wishes, but I do not know how to do this nor have I ever heard of such a skill, and I have only one day left," he said.

The girl thought for a while and then said: "Don't be sad, father. I will try to make the suit shine," and she set off to work.

She scraped the mother-of-pearl off twenty-three shells and mixed it in water. Then she took the suit and soaked it for several hours and hung it up to dry under the stars.

Next morning the suit sparkled like the stars, so the tailor brought the suit to the Prince, and he was impressed. He wanted to know, how the tailor had made it shine. The tailor was an honest man, so he said it was not he who deserved praise, but no one else than his young daughter.

"Who is your daughter?" asked the Prince.

"She's the shell girl," he murmured.

"Then I would like to see her."

But the islanders who happened to stand nearby said: "Why would a Prince want to see her? She's only the shell girl; a poor worker, who owns nothing more than the old scruffy clothes on her body."

Nevertheless, the Prince was determined to see the girl. So the tailor went home and sent his daughter, the shell girl, to meet the Prince at the shore. And when she stood in front of the Prince he was very surprised, for he found her very beautiful and fell in love with her. But he didn't want to show how he felt. Instead he asked her:

"Was it you who made the blue suit shine like the stars?" She shook her head and answered: "Your Majesty, I've only done a small part. It was the work of the mother--of-pearl and the stars that made the blue material shine, for I can do nothing on my own."

Then he asked her how she had done it, and when she explained to him how she had scraped off the mother-of-pearl from twenty-three shells and mixed it in blue coloured water, soaked the suit in the mixture and then hung it up under the stars to dry, he said: "You are very clever."

Then he asked her from where she had the shells, and when she told him how she'd been collecting a large chest full of shells, for seven years, he said: "You are very industrious."

Then he wanted to know what she was going to do with her collection of shells, and she answered, she'd like to share them with the children of the world who do not live on such an island and never get to see such pretty shells. But she also mentioned that she never had a chance to leave the island.

The Prince said: "You are very kindhearted. I would like to take you with me on my ship, and you may share the shells with the children of the world, for it is soon Christmas."

The girl was very happy when she heard this. But she was embarrassed to travel with a handsome Prince in her ragged clothes. Besides that, she was sad for having to leave her father behind.

"I need to go and see my father before I leave, and change my clothes," she said.

The Prince agreed and added: "When you return, wear a dress that shines as bright as the sun, so I can recognise you from afar."

The shell girl nodded, but also mentioned, it would take until tomorrow noon.

Now a neighbour of the shell girl—a jealous mother with a lazy, ugly daughter—had overheard the conversation between the Prince and the shell girl and how the shell girl had made the suit shine. She hurried to the tailor's house, before the shell girl was back, and stole twenty three shells with mother-of-pearl from the large chest.

The neighbour then scurried home and told her daughter that she should go on the Prince's ship instead of the shell girl. The ugly daughter was more than pleased to carry out her mother's wicked plan, and they set off to work as fast as they could. They scraped off the mother-of-pearl from the twenty-three stolen shells, mixed it in yellow coloured water then soaked a yellow dress in the mixture for less than an hour and hung it up at the fire-place, and sure enough, the yellow dress soon shone golden, like the sun. When it was dry, the ugly girl put on the dress and the jealous mother covered her daughter's face with a veil and told her not to reveal her face until dusk.

In the mean time, the shell girl had gone to

her father and asked for a white dress which her mother had put aside for her, long ago, before she had died. Her father had kept it all these years in a separate chest, for the day when she should become a bride. Now it was time to bring it out. But when the girl searched in her large chest for shells with mother-of-pearl, she found that many were missing, and she wondered who could have taken them.

Desperate and sad, she didn't know what to do, for it would take her several weeks to find twenty-three shells with mother-of-pearl and the Prince wanted to leave very soon.

When the Prince saw a young girl coming to the shore, wearing a yellow dress that shone like the sun, he was happy, because he thought it was the shell girl returning earlier than expected. But when she was close, he was surprised to find her face covered by a veil. Nevertheless, he took her on his ship and left the island.

The shell girl's heart was filled with sorrow when she found out that the ship had left without her, for she had fallen in love with the Prince, who had been so kind to her.

Meanwhile, on board the ship, the dress of

the false girl had started to fade. And when it was dusk, the girl took down her veil. When her face was uncovered the Prince asked her, where the chest of shells were. And the false girl answered:

"I have left them at home, for they are of no use at all."

Then he asked her, why the shine on her dress had faded away. "That is because the sun has set and it is soon night," she said.

The Prince's heart was filled with sadness and guilt as he realised that he had taken the wrong girl on his ship and that his true love was left behind. He ordered the ship to go back as quick as possible. When he arrived at the island, he went to the tailor's house and found his shell girl sitting at the workshop table, in the white dress her mother had left her, her face buried in her hands. As soon as she noticed the Prince, her face lit up and shone brighter than the sun.

He fell on his knees and asked her, if she would marry him and she answered: "Yes, with all my heart!" So this time he brought the right bride on his ship.

When her father had heard of the engage-ment, his heart filled with joy. But being old and fragile, his life on earth had come to an end, and he fell into a deep sleep only to wake up again in heaven.

The shell girl had taken the large chest with her on board, and during the twelve days of Christmas she shared the shells with the children of the world and made their eyes lighten up with joy.

The Prince brought the shell girl to his kingdom where they soon married and became a good King and Queen. As for the jealous mother and her ugly daughter—they couldn't stand the sight of shells for the rest of their lives.

THE LITTLE TAILOR AND THE

THREE WALNUTS

Once upon a time there was a poor tailor. Even though he worked hard from morning till night, he never made a fortune. All his money went towards the rent of his little home, where he lived and worked and received customers, and never did he have a penny left over. There was only enough for one satisfying meal a day. So one late autumn day he said to himself: "What am I working for so hard? I don't see any sense in working hard and not getting anywhere. And besides that, I am quite lonely. I will go away to discover the world and to seek my fortune!"

But even as he spoke, the tailor started to pack his few belongings in a large handkerchief: A grand suit made of red velvet he had tailored himself, three walnuts from the tree next to his home, his food bowl, a needle and thread. He cut off a strong stick from the nut tree, which had kept his home shady in summer. Then he tied the cloth to the end of the stick, swung it onto his shoulder and closed the door behind him. Just as he was about to leave, he heard a voice calling his name. But when he turned around, he couldn't see anyone, so he shrugged his shoulders and left. Just then the voice sounded again. The tailor stopped and went to the nut tree, from where the voice came from.

"You must know, that I am not a usual tree," it said. "And the three nuts you are taking with on your journey, also not. Because you have been so hard working they shall help you when you are in need."

The tailor didn't quite know what it meant, but he didn't ponder for long and went on his way.

After walking through fields and villages, towards evening he came to a forest and felt very hungry. There he heard the sound of an axe hitting against wood, and when he came closer, to his surprise he discovered a giant who was trying to cut down an enormous fir tree.

The tailor pulled out the bowl and the needle from the towel and said to the giant: "If you fill my bowl with food, I will show you how to cut the tree with this thin needle."

The giant laughed at him and said what a fool the tailor was. He'd been working hard for over an hour, trying to cut down the tree, and was only half way through. And now this little chap was claiming he would cut down the tree with the help of a thin needle only. But our little tailor insisted, and so the giant went to fetch bread and cheese from his cave and gave it to him. But while the tailor ate happily, the giant thought about how to lure the tailor into his cave, because he planned to have him for his breakfast next day. He also didn't want to miss out the fun of watching the foolish tailor trying to fell the fir tree with a needle.

After the tailor was content with eating bread and cheese, he thought about how to get himself out of his trouble, for he had no idea, how to cut a tree with a thin needle. Just then he remembered the nuts. As soon as he held one in his hand, he understood the language of the birds.

One sparrow chirped to the other: "Oh, if

only the poor tailor knew! Soon a strong wind will blow. He only needs to stick the needle in the tree and the wind will do the rest."

The nut rolled out of his hand and vanished among the leaves. Then he sprang up and stuck the needle in the tree. Soon, a strong wind started to blow and pushed the tree down with a loud crash.

The giant was impressed and pondered over what had happened. He felt cheated, but because he wanted to take advantage of the tailor, he asked him to stay overnight in his cave, since it was getting dark soon.

The tailor gladly accepted the invitation, for he didn't have a roof over his head anymore, and wouldn't have known any other place to stay.

In the cave it was dark and creepy. But because it was stormy outside, our tailor thought it still better than being exposed to wind and rain.

The giant made a fire in the cave and put a big pot over it, and the tailor asked him, what he was preparing. The giant answered: "I am preparing a stew; if you have something for the stew, you can throw it in!"

Then he stirred the stew and mumbled:

"Stir the stew and make it good, add the meat and chop the wood!"

The tailor wondered about this, but the only provisions he had were the nuts, and as soon as he held one in his hand, he understood the language of the stones. And they said: "Oh, if only the poor tailor knew what the gi-ant is planning! Today at midnight he will kill him with his axe and eat him in the stew."

Now the tailor understood why he found it creepy in the cave. First he lay down in the bed, which the giant had offered him, but as soon as he heard the giant snoring he crept into a corner, close to the cave entrance. The walnut rolled away through the entrance into the darkness. Then he heard the giant get up and chop the bed apart with three blows of his axe, and then go back to sleep again.

At the crack of dawn the tailor slipped out of the cave and with fresh courage went on his way. When the giant noticed that the tailor had cheated him, he cursed so loud, one could hear it far and wide.

But our little tailor had already arrived in the mountains, far off where he met a group of funny little men with beards and flat hats. They were busy pulling up an iron tub, half filled with gold and precious stones on a rope, out of a deep mine.

The little tailor watched them with interest for a while when the worn rope suddenly ripped through, due to the weight of the gold and precious stones, and the tub fell with its content to the bottom of the mine. The tailor was hungry again and just then an idea came into his mind. He unpacked the bowl and thread from his towel and said:

"If you fill my bowl with food, I will show you how I can pull up the tub—filled to the rim—just with this thread. And if I succeed, you shall give me a handful of the gold and a handful of the precious stones!"

The dwarfs laughed at him. "Foolish fellow!" they cried. "How can you pull up the whole weight of a tub filled with gold and precious stones by a thin thread. Alright, daredevil, you shall go down and we will see what awaits you!"

"But first give me some food!" the tailor demanded.

So the dwarfs fetched bread and cheese and the tailor ate until he was full up. Then they pushed him down into the deep mine, where he hurt his arms and legs from the impact of the fall. Now the poor lad really didn't know what to do. In his misery he remembered the third nut, which he was carrying in his trouser pocket. As soon as he held it in his hand, he heard deep voices. It was the roots that reached down into the mine that spoke:

"Oh, if only the tailor knew that the earth would soon split up and push the tub to the surface! He just needs to tie his thread to the handle and the earth will do the rest."

Then the third walnut rolled away into the darkness of the mine, and he never saw it again.

It started grumbling under the earth and the tailor quickly tied the thread around the handle and before he knew it, the earth split up and the tub, along with himself were pushed up to the surface of the earth.

The dwarfs who had fallen onto their backs due to the earthquake, were very surprised when they found the tailor with the full tub. They gave him a handful of gold and a handful of precious stones, as arranged. Now the tailor could afford to get his own food, since one little piece of gold lasted a long time.

Our tailor went on his way and after many days—it was towards the end of Advent—he came to a town. Here he heard that the king wished to have his daughter married to a young prince. But the princess had put up a difficult condition: She would only marry the one who could give her a Christmas present, which would give her lasting joy.

The princess was a very spoilt young girl who had everything she wanted. But her joy lasted only a short while after she received something. The king took her wish very serious and threatened any suitor to chop off his head if he did not succeed with fulfilling her wish.

Our tailor therefore put on his Sunday suit, which he had carried around in his handkerchief all the while. It was as nice as on the day he had sewed it. Then he filled one pocket with gold and the other one with precious stones.

As he stood in front of the king in his red velvet suit, the king thought he was presented with a prince and said: "You have three days: Three times you are allowed to offer my daughter a present. But if her joy doesn't last, you will lose your head!"

The little tailor nodded and answered: "Yes, your Majesty! I will certainly make your daughter's happiness last!"

On the first day, when the tailor saw the princess, he offered her a handful of gold. Her eyes lit up from seeing the gold but soon faded again, and she just shook her head and sulked.

The next day, he offered her a handful of beautiful gems sparkling in all colours. The princess looked at them shortly, turned up her nose and expelled a rude word. The tailor thought to himself: "This princess is truly spoilt. And besides she's also sulky." But when he looked into her pretty face and in her eyes, it appeared to him, that she was looking sad.

So he said: "I expected you would not like these treasures. But just wait until tomorrow, then you will bid farewell to your sadness!" Then he noticed her glancing at him lovingly and hopefully which made him think that it would be a real shame if he could not have her as his wife!

Through the whole night he pondered over how he could give the princess a lasting joy, and the longer he thought about it, the more he noticed how important the princess had become to him. His heart was so full of affection, that he thought it would burst, if he couldn't give her the right present. At the same time he became very desperate, because he didn't have any more walnuts that could help him.

In his biggest distress, he remembered what his mother had told him a long time ago:

"If you ever are in great need, pray to your guardian angel. He'll help you!"

So our tailor prayed to his guardian angel and as soon as he had finished the short prayer, a bright white light appeared shining brighter than the sun. And a voice spoke: "Oh, if only you knew: Today the Infant Jesus will come down to earth, just as on the day of his birth. When the princess sees him, joy will never again leave her."

The tailor quickly asked where and how he and the princess could get there. And the angel explained, he would have to be at such and such a place, at such and such a time. Then the light vanished and the tailor found he was alone in the dark once more. However, the tailor was now filled with confidence.

When the sun rose on Christmas morning, the tailor hurried to the castle and told the princess, that he was going to offer her his last present. She should come to such and such a place—it wouldn't be far. As the tailor reached the edge of the forest with his princess accompanied by the king's soldiers, he discovered a hole up in the cave, and said to the princess: "There is the present you'll never get tired of!"

Then the tailor saw how the princess held her breath and sank to her knees and he wondered why. In the cave were a very beautiful woman and a young man with wise eyes bending over a crib. In the crib was the Infant Christ, surrounded by a heavenly glow. The child smiled at the princess. But only the princess could see all this. Yet the tailor noticed how the princess beamed all over her face and how tears of joy ran down her cheeks.

Now the tailor knew that his princess had found lasting joy, and he couldn't wait to marry her.

When the king found out that the tailor was not a prince, he became angry. But he wasn't allowed to break his promise, because it was never mentioned, that only a prince was allowed to marry the princess. So he said to the tailor:

"There is a dangerous dragon in the dark forest. You have to kill it, before you get my daughter for a wife. And you better bring me the dragon's split tongue as a proof that you have killed it!"

So the little tailor went off once more, but didn't know how to manage this task, because he had neither a sword, nor did he know anything about dragon fighting. And so he called upon his guardian angel once more. But this time the guardian angel didn't appear, and so the tailor went on his way feeling sad. Soon he met a smith, and the tailor begged him to forge a sword. The smith said: "If you are prepared to give me your whole fortune, then I will make a sword with which you will overpower the dragon once and for all."

The tailor thought to himself: "Indeed, I do have a fortune—plenty of gold and precious stones, but they are not that precious to me. They can't even make the princess happy." So he gave his whole fortune to the smith. The smith was really his guardian angel in disguise. And he forged the sword out of the gold and gems, a kind of sword that no one had ever seen or held in their hands before.

Now the tailor found the cave in the forest and challenged the dragon to come out. And with his miraculous sword the dragon soon lay dead at the tailor's feet. The little tailor cut out the dragon's split tongue and brought it to the king as proof. Now the king had no more excuses and gave the tailor to his daughter. She was very happy, because she had long recognized that the tailor was a clever lad with a good heart. So they soon celebrated their wedding and both lived happily ever after.

As for the three walnuts, in each place where they rolled to, a new nut tree grew that bore fruits for a thousand years.

THE BEAUTY CONTEST

Once upon a time the Judge of the World announced a competition among the virtues. The most beautiful one would get a special prize: She would be the first to visit the infant Jesus.

Because everyone knew that the birth of the Redeemer was something unique, they all wanted to win this contest. The judge then invited these virtues to participate: Love, Faith, Hope, Justice, Wisdom, Fortitude, Moderation and lastly Humbleness.

When the devil heard he was not invited, jealousy made him turn yellow and green and he complained vociferously to the Judge. But the judge just answered: "What kind of beauty do you represent to this world? None at all! Go away, you evil swindler, I don't want to see you anymore!"

This answer got the devil hopping mad and

he drew up a plan, how he could take revenge. Then he sent off his small but zealous Demon of Pride and told him to bite each virtue into their right shoulder. More than that he couldn't do, because he didn't possess the power to kill them.

It then happened that the small Demon of Pride bit the right shoulders of the virtues; all except Humbleness, for neither the devil nor the little demon expected Humbleness to have been invited. They thought she was too simple-minded.

When the competition took place, one virtue after the other stepped before the judge and he looked at them thoroughly.

First the virtue of Love came forward, and the judge said: "You would be very beautiful indeed, but when you gave something away lately, you were thinking more of your own glory, than of the receiver."

Next it was Faith's turn and the judge said: "You would be very beautiful indeed, but recently, because of your faith, you were behaving arrogantly towards others!"

When it was Hope's turn, the judge said: "You would be very beautiful indeed, but recently you flattered Despair, and that I do not like at all."

And so it went on. The judge found something wrong with every virtue until it was Humbleness' turn. She felt ashamed to stand before the judge because she did not find herself worthy of participating in the beauty contest. But she didn't mention anything and was sure that the judge would find something wrong about her.

To the surprise of everyone, the judge said to Humbleness:

"You are truly the most beautiful of all virtues, for you have been entirely free of pride. But watch out for the small Demon of Pride and make sure he never bites you, otherwise the same will happen to you, as to the others."

As a prize for her beauty, Humbleness was the first to visit the newborn king.

And so it happened that apart from the Blessed Virgin Mary and Saint Joseph, the shepherds were the first ones to adore the infant Jesus, because they were the humblest of all!

The Unexpected Guest

During the whole week I had waited for this day. At last Saturday evening had arrived, and as usual, I went to my Grandmother's house.

Babunia, as we called her, lived with Granddad in a small wooden hut. I opened the iron garden gate and walked along a straight path between large potato beds, that were now covered with a thin layer of snow, leading up to the door. Before knocking on the door I paused for a moment and admired the colourful flowers painted on the white background of the front wall, and also the swirling patterns carved into the wooden door frame. Without awaiting an answer, I entered. Babunia stood bent over the stove and said:

"Come over, my dear. The tea is still hot." Then she poured the steaming liquid from a metal kettle into my mug.

Babunia had a round face and red cheeks. She had small sparkly eyes, and when she smiled, they vanished in a sea of wrinkles. Her silver-grey, long hair was always tied up in a bun, and her kind look warmed my heart. I always found it hard to imagine Babunia as a young girl, nor that she would one day not be around anymore.

Babunia could neither read nor write, but she could tell stories which I loved listening to.

Granddad piled on wood through the little opening in the stove. It crackled and the light of the flickering yellow flame reflected on his face. I stepped closer to watch the lively spectacle of the flames.

The warmth coming from the stove was enough to keep the whole hut warm, which contained just a single room and a kitchen.

Granddad sat on a chair at the stove, under a crucifix, that hung on the wall. He was a quiet man and short grown, like Grandmother.

Dziadek—that is how we called him—was always present, when Babunia told her stories. He held his walking stick in his hands and supported his chin on it and remained silent, shuffling his black heavy leather shoes now and then, or nodding his head approvingly. When she had finished her tale, he would look thoughtfully.

Babunia sat on her chair at the table, and I next to her on the bench. She rested her arms on the worn-off wood.

Usually she would tell of fearsome dragons, brave knights and fair princesses, of dwarfs, elves and fairies. But once during Advent, she told a story that I will always remember:

"When I was as small as you," she started, "this is what happened:

At that time there lived a mother with five children in this village. Their father had died in the war and the widow was rather poor. The family lived very modestly and had to turn over every grosz four times before spending it.

It was Christmas Eve and the daughters helped their mother prepare a modest, yet special supper. One of them laid the table. Apart from the six family member she also added a cover for the Grandparents, an aunt and uncle and their three children, who were expected to join. The family had a long table with space for everyone, although they had to

34

move closely together.

The widow, a pious woman, who regularly visited holy mass in the small wooden church, asked her daughter to lay a spare plate.

'But mother, that is hardly possible,' the daughter said. 'There is barely any space for us thirteen people!'

But the woman insisted and even pointed out that the spare space should be at the head of the table, where otherwise the father would be seated, if he had still been here. As a matter of fact, it was a pious custom to leave a spare space for an unexpected guest at the table on Christmas Eve.

Shaking her head the girl obeyed.

When the whole family, grandparents, sister-in-law with her husband and their children were merrily gathered around the table and the hosts started serving pastry pockets filled with fresh cheese, sauerkraut stew and beetroot soup, suddenly there was a loud knock on the door. And as the oldest son went to the door and opened it, there in front of him stood an old beggar in the wind and snow, and he asked to be let in.

At first he didn't want to let him in, and suggested he'd go the priest, who lived in the next road. But the housewife said he must let the man in.

So the stranger trudged in and the merry party became silent, as they watched the poor man enter. He was wearing several layers of ragged clothes to defy the cold and was slightly bent. His feet were clad in shoes full of holes and with the soles coming off.

But the woman offered him the empty seat at the table, took his stick and tattered hat and said:

'We haven't got much, but whatever we have, we're willing to share. It is certainly pleasanter than outside in the darkness and drifting snow.'

This good woman filled the spare plate with the same food, that had been prepared for her own family and their guests.

The poor man ate slowly and didn't say a word, holding the spoon tightly with his hand red from the cold. One could see that he hadn't been eating such good food for a long time, for he marvelled at everything, his eyes shimmering with tears.

Because he was so quiet, the others soon turned back to their own food and continued with socialising.

When dinner was over, and some family members and guests had sung Christmas carols, whilst others enjoyed hot compote and sweet pastry, the beggar stood up, as if he was about to leave.

But as soon as he stood, his bent back seemed to straighten; and suddenly he wasn't a bent beggar anymore in ragged clothes, but a young man in a long, white, clean robe. He held up his right hand in a blessing gesture and vanished from everyone's sight.

Then the woman, her family and guests knew, it was the Saviour himself, who had stopped at their home, on this very Christmas Eve. Full of wonder they attended the Midnight Mass told everyone what had happened.

On Christmas Day the village priest blessed the house as well as the place, where our Saviour had been seated. Much later, on the spot where this house stood, a chapel was built and people say, that their village is blessed. None of the inhabitants had to suffer from severe hunger ever since. White lilies grew out of the stick that the beggar had left behind; and the hat and stick were brought to Rome, where pilgrims can still view it."

How Robin Redbreast

Brought the Christmas Tree

At a gathering in Advent, the King of the birds gave some of his subjects a special task. The sparrow was to twitter the latest news, the eagle was to soar in the mountain areas and help the lost and injured, the cock would wake up the farmer early in the morning, and the pigeons would clear up the crumbs, people dropped in front of the Cathedral.

Little Robin waited eagerly for his special task, but nothing happened. He was so disappointed and angry, his head turned red, and he suppressed his feelings, so they slipped down and coloured his breast a glowing red.

This hadn't escaped the Kings eyes. He turned to Robin and said: "Do you really want everyone to call you 'Robin Redbreast' for being angry?"

At that little Robin blushed, the red colour moved up and his chest went brown again.

"Your majesty," replied the Robin. "I'd prefer to be known for hard working, rather than for being angry."

The King thought for a while. He knew that Robin was an eager and strong-willed bird, and so he came up with an idea.

"Robin! I have a special task for you," he announced. "On Christmas Eve, you shall bring a fir tree into people's homes. This kind of tree shall be called a Christmas tree and will be adorned with pretty things. The sight of the Christmas tree shall warm up people's hearts, especially the children's, because Christmas is a time to rejoice! Since you're not flying to Africa during winter, you are the perfect one to fulfil this task."

So Robin gathered his kinfolk and told them, what the King had announced and they soon set off to work. They gathered pretty things from all over the country, flew to the forest, and chose a dozen of the finest fir trees. They hung up golden coloured fir cones and silver coloured walnuts on the twigs and tied on red and yellow ribbons and in the end added white candles. Soon the fir trees shone in full glory.

On Christmas Eve, when they had finished decorating, each robin took a tip of ribbon in its beak, and the woodpeckers came to cut the trees. The king of the birds breathed on the robins and a special strength got hold of them, and so they flew with the Christmas trees to peoples' homes.

The King of the birds praised their good work and the people rejoiced and admired the beautiful Christmas trees.

From working so hard the Robins' chests started to glow red, the red colour even went up to their neck and face and stayed there. So all Robins are named Robin Redbreast ever since.

Nowadays it's hard to find Robins still bringing Christmas trees, but you will occasionally discover a Robin on a Christmas card, and some folks stick a few artificial robin redbreasts onto their decorated Christmas tree.

Printed in Great Britain
by Amazon